Art Queen

by Marci Peschke

illustrated by Tuesday Mourning

PICTURE WINDOW BOOKS
a capstone imprint

Kylie Jean is published by Picture Window Books
A Capstone Imprint
1710 Roe Crest Drive
North Mankato, Minnesota 56003
www.mycapstone.com

Library of Congress Cataloging-in-Publication Data
Cataloging-in-Publication information is on file with the Library of Congress.
Names: Peschke, Marci, author. | Mourning, Tuesday, illustrator.
Title: Art Queen
ISBN 978-1-5158-2927-0 (library binding)
ISBN 978-1-5158-2935-5 (paper over board)
ISBN 978-1-5158-2931-7 (eBook PDF)

Creative Director: Nathan Gassman
Graphic Designer: Sarah Bennett
Editor: Shelly Lyons
Production Specialist: Kris Wilfahrt

Design Elements: Shutterstock

Printed and bound in Canada.
PA020

For Tuesday, Art Queen
Artist Extraordinaire—MP

Table of Contents

All About Me, Kylie Jean!......................7

Chapter One
Pretty as a Picture...........................11

Chapter Two
Art Club Contest...............................23

Chapter Three
The Pink Kylie..................................34

Chapter Four
Puppy Portrait..................................45

Chapter Five
Pop Art Kylie....................................58

Chapter Six
Watercolor Washout............................ 66

Chapter Seven
Abstract Kylie...76

Chapter Eight
Show and Tell...82

Chapter Nine
Gallery Walk 91

Chapter Ten
Minimalist Kylie Jean........................100

All About Me, Kylie Jean!

My name is Kylie Jean Carter. I live in a big, sunny, yellow house on Peachtree Lane in Jacksonville, Texas, with Momma, Daddy, and my two brothers, T.J. and Ugly Brother.

T.J. is my older brother, and Ugly Brother is . . . well . . . he's really a dog. Don't you go telling him he is a dog. Okay? I mean it. He thinks he is a real true person.

He is a black-and-white bulldog. His front looks like his back, all smashed in. His face is all droopy like he's sad, but he's not.

His two front teeth stick out, and his tongue hangs down. (Now you know why his name is Ugly Brother.)

Everyone I love to the moon and back lives in Jacksonville. Nanny, Pa, Granny, Pappy, my aunts, my uncles, and my cousins all live here. I'm extra lucky, because I can see all of them any time I want to!

My momma says I'm pretty. She says I have eyes as blue as the summer sky and a smile as sweet as an angel. (Momma says pretty is as pretty does. That means being nice to the old folks, taking care of little animals, and respecting my momma and daddy.)

But I'm pretty on the outside and on the inside. My hair is long, brown, and curly.

I wear it in a ponytail sometimes, but my absolute most favorite is when Momma pulls it back in a princess style on special days.

I just gave you a little hint about my big dream. Ever since I was a bitty baby I have wanted to be an honest-to-goodness beauty queen. I even know the wave. It's side to side, nice and slow, with a dazzling smile. I practice all the time, because everybody knows beauty queens need to have a perfect wave.

I'm Kylie Jean, and I'm going to be a beauty queen. Just you wait and see!

Chapter One
Pretty as a Picture

I sleepily roll over to the sound of my pillow crunching. It's the sound of paper. Tucked under my pillow is an invitation to a special party. I bounce out of bed. My dog, Ugly Brother, follows me.

It's Saturday, and tonight Daddy and I are going to the opening of the Cooper County College yearly art exhibit. Daddy got invited because he is writing a story about local artists for the paper.

Poor Momma, she can't go because she's away at a quilting retreat all weekend. Daddy says they open the exhibit with a fancy party. Since Momma isn't here, he'd be honored to take his other favorite girl. That's me!

Ugly Brother wants to go too, but he can't. I know he's sad.

"After breakfast, would you like to help me pick out a dress for the party?" I ask him.

He barks, "Ruff, ruff!"

Two barks means yes. He follows me downstairs to the kitchen.

"No bacon today," I tell him. "Would you like a bowl of cereal instead?"

He barks, "Ruff, ruff!"

He eats anything. I get a bowl out of the cabinet for me, and I use Ugly Brother's doggie bowl for him. Then I pour us both cereal and milk. We like peanut butter cereal best. I tell him that after breakfast we can have a little fashion show.

After breakfast, we hurry back upstairs. I look through my closet and pick out several dresses. "Are you ready to help me choose a dress?" I ask Ugly Brother.

"Ruff, ruff," he replies.

Then he jumps up and down excitedly. I try on all the dresses and model them for Ugly Brother. When I show him my hot pink mini dress with the big white polka dots, he goes crazy, chasing his tail and barking. I look in my tall mirror.

Yup, I look glamorous! This dress is perfect for a grown-up party. I set it out on my bed for later.

The rest of the day drags by. I can't wait to go to the party! In the afternoon, I fix my hair in a little bun on top of my head, just like Momma taught me. But then I change my mind and decide to wear my hair down around my shoulders.

Then I sit on my bed to read and wait for dinner.

Finally, Daddy calls me down to eat. "Dinnertime, sugar!" he yells from downstairs.

I jump up and run toward the stairs. "Coming!" I yell.

Daddy and T.J. are already sitting at the table. I take a seat next to T.J.

Daddy made hamburgers with curly fries. It's one of his specialties. T.J. eats two burgers!

"Daddy, this burger is delicious, and your curly fries just gave me an idea," I tell him.

"Thank you, sugar," replied Daddy. "What are you going to do with curly fries?"

"I don't need the fries," I say, "but I'm going to make curls in my ponytail! After dinner, can you please help me with the curling iron?"

"Sure!" says Daddy. "You tell me where you want the curls, and I'll curl your ponytail. We'll make a great team."

"Speaking of teams," T.J. says, "I'm meeting the guys. I'll see y'all later." He puts his plate in the dishwasher and turns toward the door.

"Don't stay out too late," Daddy tells him.

"Don't worry, I won't!" T.J. says.

Daddy and I clean up our dishes before going to get the curling iron. Daddy curls my hair, and then I put on my dress.

"Don't you look chic!" says Daddy.

"Thanks, Daddy. You look handsome too!"

"Thanks, sugar," he says as he smiles.

As we head for the door, Ugly Brother runs up with our invitation hanging from his mouth.

"Thank you, boy!" Daddy says as he pats him on the head an grabs the invitation.

Ugly Brother barks, "Ruff, ruff."

At the college, Daddy parks the truck, opens my door, and gives me his arm. He's a true gentleman. Together we walk toward the art department.

Through the large glass windows, the gallery glows. Inside, college students pass out punch and delicious little snacks on silver trays. One of the snacks has bacon on it, so I wrap it in a napkin and slip it in my pocket for Ugly Brother.

We stroll around looking at all the wonderful art. It's AMAZING!

"Some of the paintings are done by students," Daddy tells me. "But others are on loan to the college from famous museums."

"Oh . . . look at this one!" I cry as I point to a painting on the wall behind him.

It's a picture of a beautiful lady with a black braid in the back. She has a bird on her shoulder. I love it!

"That is lovely," says Daddy. Then he turns away to ask one of the artists some questions for his article.

"I agree!" I say as I lean a little closer to the painting.

I am trying to read about the picture of the beautiful lady when I hear a familiar voice behind me. I turn around to see my art teacher, Mr. Lee.

"Well, hello, Kylie Jean!" says Mr. Lee.

"Hi, Mr. Lee," I reply.

"Do you like the painting by Frida Kahlo?" he asks, pointing to the painting of the beautiful lady with the black hair.

"I love it! Especially the bright colors," I tell him.

"You have a good eye for art!" he tells me. "Frida was a famous artist from Mexico."

"Thank you very much," I say.

Mr. Lee adds, "If you're interested in art, you should join Art Club. It's on Mondays after school. Think about it, and ask your parents if you may join the club."

"Art Club sounds really cool," I reply. "I'll ask my parents."

"Great," he says. "See you at school."

I look for Daddy. He's still talking to the artist. I can't wait to tell him about Art Club. I'm looking at a statue of a cowboy when Daddy walks up.

"I think I've asked enough questions for one night!" he says. "Hopefully I have all of the information I need to write my story."

"I have a question for you!" I blurt out. "Can I join my school's art club? My art teacher, Mr. Lee, is here, and he asked me if I'd like to join."

"I'm happy to be answering a question instead of asking one," says Daddy. "Yes! I think Art Club sounds fantastic."

I give Daddy a big squeezy hug. "Yay! And thank you, thank you!"

"You're welcome, sugar. Now, we should head home," says Daddy.

On the way home, I think about Frida and the beautiful painting of the woman with the braid.

Before I know it, we're back home. Daddy opens the door, and I make my way upstairs to get ready for bed.

"Thanks for a great night," I tell Daddy.

"You're welcome. Thanks for being a great date!" Daddy replies.

Before I go to bed, I give Ugly Brother the bacon snack from my pocket. While I braid my hair in one long braid, I tell him about the famous Frida.

Frida Kahlo was a famous Mexican artist who painted many self-portraits.

Chapter Two
Art Club Contest

On Monday morning, I remind Momma that I have permission to stay after school for Art Club.

Momma warns, "Eat your breakfast, Kylie Jean, or you'll miss the bus!"

"Okie dokie," I tell her.

Momma adds, "Of course I remember about Art Club! You can't stop talking about the club and Mr. Lee. It sounds like fun."

Just then we hear the honk, HONK of the bus horn. My favorite bus driver, Mr. Jim, is here to pick me up. Momma was right, I'm late!

I run to the door, grabbing my backpack and lunch box. "Bye, Momma! Love you!"

She shouts back, "Bye! Love you too!"

I climb up the bus steps. My best cousin, Lucy, has been saving my seat in the first row, right behind Mr. Jim.

"Hey, Lucy, and good morning, Mr. Jim," I sing.

Lucy looks up and says, "Hi."

Mr. Jim says, "You're running late today, little gal!"

"Sorry, Mr. Jim," I reply as I sit down next to Lucy. "I won't be riding the bus home this afternoon. I have a special invitation to join a club!"

Lucy asks, "What club are you joining?"

"Mr. Lee asked me to join Art Club," I tell her.

"Will you paint?" asks Lucy.

"I think I'll make all kinds of art," I say.

"That sounds fun!" says Lucy. "Speaking of paint, I'm getting new paint for my bedroom. Can you come help paint on Thursday after school?"

"Sure!" I reply.

All morning, I can't stop thinking about art. At lunchtime in the cafeteria, one of the older girls hears me talking to Lucy about Art Club.

"Hey, my name is Georgia," says the girl as she stops by our table. "I'm in Art Club too. What's your name?"

"I'm Kylie Jean," I tell her.

"See you later, Kylie Jean," she says.

Lucy says, "That's awesome! Now you'll have a new friend in the club."

I nod and finish my sandwich. After lunch, we have recess, science, and P.E. I'm so anxious to get to Art Club that I don't even have fun stacking cups in P.E.

When the last bell rings, I give Lucy a quick hug and head to the bathroom to change out of my nice dress. I put on jeans and a plain pink T-shirt for painting. Then I walk to the art room.

The sign on the art room door says "Art Studio." The room is big with wide, sunny windows and lots of interesting things to look at. I see a big bowl of fruit, a large horse statue painted indigo blue, and several vases of giant sunflowers. I also see Georgia waving at me.

"Hi," I say as I take the seat next to her.

"Hi, Kylie Jean," says Georgia. She gives me a big smile.

I set down my backpack. As I look around, I think I might be the youngest kid here, but then I see Ryder. He's in second grade too!

Mr. Lee walks to the front of the room. "Welcome to Art Club, everyone!" he says.

He turns on his projector and shows us a picture of a woman with flowers. There's a lot of blue in this painting!

"The name of this painting is *Jacqueline with Flowers*," he says, "and the artist is Pablo Picasso. Picasso was a famous Spanish artist. For several years, he painted pictures using only blue and green paint with little touches of other colors. This was called his Blue Period. Today you will each create your own blue painting."

Mr. Lee gives each student a large piece of art paper. Down the middle of the table are cups of blue paint in all different shades, from pale robin's egg blue to deep midnight blue. There are also palette trays filled with other colors.

Mr. Lee says, "Remember to use the extra colors only for accents. Your painting should be mostly shades of blue."

I look at the large white piece of paper. I'm not sure what to paint.

Georgia is inspired! She starts painting right away. I see she is painting a lady with flowers like Picasso did. It's not the same lady, but it's good. She's a talented artist.

I look over at Ryder. "What are you going to paint?" I ask.

He says, "I like that blue horse."

I decide that if Ryder is painting something in the room, I can too! I choose to paint blue sunflowers in a vase. I use the indigo blue paint. Instead of painting Mr. Lee's vase, I paint a blue and white vase like Granny has. It's my favorite vase!

Mr. Lee walks by and stops next to me. "Kylie Jean, that vase is beautiful," he says. "Do you have one like it at home?"

"My granny has one," I tell him.

"You are using your artist's eye again," he tells me. "Good for you."

When we are all done, we leave our paintings on the drying rack. Then it's time to clean up. I start picking up brushes and paint trays. Georgia and the other kids do the same.

Mr. Lee says, "Artists always take care of their materials!"

We wash our brushes and carefully put away our leftover paint. When everything is cleaned up, Mr. Lee has a special announcement.

"I'm pleased and excited to announce that the school is having a mural art contest!" he tells us.

"What's a mural?" I ask him.

"Great question," he says. "A mural is a very large painting that covers an entire wall or building. You will create your ideas with watercolor paint. If you win the contest, your art will be used to paint a mural on the wall at the entrance of the school. To prepare for the contest, our club will meet on Mondays, Wednesdays, and Fridays for the next two weeks."

Everyone starts talking all at once, asking questions. It's so loud and noisy that it sounds like a school bus. Mr. Lee answers our questions quickly because it's time to go!

Pablo Picasso was only thirteen years old
when he went to fine arts school.

T.J. picks me up from Art Club. He tells me all about football practice. His truck smells like sweat and dirty socks, and I can't wait to get home. Thankfully it's not a long drive.

Ugly Brother is waiting in the front yard. When we get there, he runs over to the driveway. I jump out and give him a big squeezy hug.

"I missed you today, and I have some exciting news!" I tell him. "I bet you missed me too!"

He barks, "Ruff, ruff."

In the kitchen, Momma and Daddy are making dinner. It smells saucy, like tomatoes.

"Are we having spaghetti?" I ask.

Momma says, "Good guess!"

Daddy looks at T.J. and tells him to go take a quick shower before dinner.

I see lettuce, tomato, and cucumber on the table beside a big bowl. I wash my hands in the kitchen sink. Then I tear the lettuce and begin making a salad.

Momma turns around. "You are the sweetest, nicest daughter in the whole wide world!" she says.

Ugly Brother barks twice and runs around the kitchen. He thinks I'm nice too!

Daddy cuts the tomato and cucumber for me and places them on top of the lettuce.

Momma calls T.J. to come to the table. We sit down, say grace, and dig in.

Over spaghetti, I share my big news! "Today at Art Club I found out my school is having a mural contest. A mural is a giant painting on a wall, in case you didn't know. I am determined to win the contest!"

T.J. asks, "How do you plan to win?"

"I'm going to work extra hard in Art Club and at home so I can learn all about different artists and art styles," I tell them. "I already know about Picasso and his Blue Period."

"That's impressive, sugar!" says Daddy.

Momma adds, "I've always loved your pictures. I can't wait to see what you paint."

As soon as I'm done eating, I ask to be excused from the table so I can paint. T.J. offers to do the dishes. I thank him and give him a big squeezy hug.

In my room, I think about Picasso and his blue paintings. I get out some art paper and the paint set and easel that Granny gave me for my birthday.

I paint for hours, until it's time to get ready for bed. Momma knocks on my door to tuck me in.

"Don't come in!" I yell. "I'm painting a surprise. Ugly Brother can tuck me in tonight."

Ugly Brother barks, "Ruff, ruff."

"OK," says Momma. "Love you!"

"Love you too!" I reply.

I get into bed. Ugly Brother gets into bed too. He pulls up my covers with his teeth and licks my face. That's his way of kissing me goodnight. He's an awesome doggie brother.

* * * *

The next day school crawls by slower than a turtle chasing a June bug. All I want to do is get home and paint. I try to pay attention to my lessons, but it's hard. Then at three o'clock the last bell rings, and I race to the bus.

When I finally get home, Momma is sitting at the kitchen table writing in a notebook.

I rush over to her side and eye the fruit bowl on the table. "Can I just have a piece of fruit for my snack?" I ask. "I need to get right to work painting!"

Momma just smiles, shrugs, and hands me an apple.

I stay in my room working until dinnertime. Momma calls us down to eat. It's a super simple supper. We're just having soup and salad to eat. After dinner I can't wait to show Momma what I've been doing.

"Can I show you my room, Momma?" I ask.

"What's going on in your room, sugar?" Momma asks me.

"I've renamed my room K.J.'s Art Studio," I tell her. "I even have a sign on the door."

We climb up the stairs, and I push open the door to my new studio. Momma steps inside and gasps in amazement. Everywhere she looks are paintings in shades of PINK! Flamingo pink flowers, Granny's house painted in shades of bubble gum and peony pink, a fuchsia horse, and my neighbor Miss Clarabelle in rose tones. As she turns to look at all of them, she sees a picture of me with a crown of pink flowers on my head.

"Oh, I love that one!" says Momma as she points at my portrait. "It's my favorite."

"That one is my self-portrait," I tell her. "I painted it in the style of Frida Kahlo. She was a famous Mexican artist."

Momma laughs and says, "If Picasso had a blue period, I think this must be your pink period! I love all of this and can't wait to see what you do next in Art Club."

"Thanks, Momma!" I say as I give her a big squeezy hug.

* * * *

The next day is Wednesday. It's another Art Club day! Mr. Lee takes us to the school library. We all check out a book about a famous artist. Ryder picks George Remington, a cowboy artist. I pick Georgia O'Keeffe, because my new friend is also named Georgia. Plus, I really like the gorgeous flower on the book's cover.

Back in the art room, Mr. Lee invites us to look through our books and choose a picture by our famous artist to recreate.

I page through my book and see paintings of flowers, desert landscapes, and cattle skulls.

Ryder asks, "Which picture did you choose, Kylie Jean?"

"I like this picture of the desert with a cattle skull and horns," I reply. "The colors are gorgeous! It reminds me of the desert in west Texas."

Ryder shows me his picture, and then I get busy with my project. First I study the painting by Georgia O'Keefe. Then I start painting a low, rusty mountain range for my background. In the front, or foreground, I paint the large skull and flowers.

Mr. Lee walks by my table. "I like your painting, Kylie Jean," he says. "Are you going to use it for the painting contest?"

"I'm not sure yet," I reply.

He shows me how to create shadows on the skull. "O'Keeffe was a modern artist because of the way she created her own style," he tells me. "She painted a lot of skulls because she found them interesting."

His words give me an idea. I can't wait to try it in my studio!

Modern art comes from artists who were trying to see art in a new way. They experimented with shape, color, scale, and subjects. They did not paint the same way artists had always painted.

Chapter Four
Puppy Portrait

Later that night after dinner, I decide to have a special talk with Ugly Brother in my room.

"I bet you didn't know you're my inspiration," I tell him as I rub his ear. "Every single morning I wake up and see your sweet puppy face. From the time I was born, you've always been around. You are smart and always doing funny things too. The famous artist Georgia O'Keeffe painted cattle skulls because she thought they were interesting."

Ugly Brother's big brown eyes look like they have little doggie tears in them.

"Don't cry! You are the most interesting dog I know!"

He gives me a wet doggie kiss on my hand.

"Would you like to be in my paintings?" I ask him as I rub his ear some more.

He wags his short, little tail and runs around the room. "Ruff, ruff," he barks.

I want a huge painting, because Georgia often painted on large canvases, so I tape four pieces of art paper together.

"Sit still!" I tell Ugly Brother. "Pretend you're a rock. You have to sit until I get your outline painted in."

He is holding so still that he doesn't even bark a reply!

"Good dog!" I say. "I'll try to hurry."

I use my small brush with black paint to make a bold outline. His ears are like little bent triangles. His flat, wrinkly face is like several ovals with a black triangle for a nose in the center. I am painting him so large that he takes up the whole center of my paper.

I put the end of my brush between my teeth and stop for a moment. I am thinking about the background of my portrait. Maybe the park would be a good background, or Uncle Bay's ranch.

But no, just then
an idea hits me like
splattered paint hitting
a canvas. Behind
him, but smaller, I
will paint the green
grass, sunflowers, and
the big red barn at
Lickskillet Farm, where
Nanny and Pa live. It
is one of our favorite
places. Ugly Brother
loves it there too!

He is starting to whine. I can tell he is tired, and
so am I. It's time for bed. Tomorrow I will finish
my puppy portrait. I brush my teeth and put on
my pajamas.

Daddy comes to tuck me in. He looks over at my big painting and asks, "Are you painting Ugly Brother?"

"Yup!" I say. "I think my doggie brother is fascinating."

Daddy laughs. "I would have to agree," he says. "He's quite a character!"

Ugly Brother licks my cheek. He knows we're talking about him.

Daddy covers me up, kisses my cheek, and pats Ugly Brother on the head.

"Love you to the moon and back!" he tells us.

"I love you a bushel and a peck and hug around the neck!" I reply. It's our special way of saying good night to each other.

I fall asleep thinking of Ugly Brother smudging pink paint on paper with his wet nose.

* * * *

In the morning before school, Momma reminds me that Aunt Susie is counting on us to come by and help paint Lucy's room in the afternoon. I run back upstairs to grab the painting I want to give Lucy for her newly-painted room. In my room, I see the painting of the pink horse. Perfect! Lucy loves little ponies!

School goes by fast! It's library day, and we have music for our special class. At lunchtime, we tell Paula and Cara all about painting Lucy's room. We are very excited.

"Painting is hard work," Cara says. "It's not really fun."

Lucy says, "We have fun whenever we are together, so we'll make it a fun painting time."

I nod and say, "Yup!"

After school, Lucy and I hop on the bus.

I ask, "Mr. Jim, can you please drop me off at Lucy's house today?"

"No, ma'am," he replies. "I'm sorry, but you have to have a note from your momma to go to Lucy's house."

I pull a piece of paper from my backpack pocket and hand it to him. "You mean like this one. Right?" I say with a grin.

He nods and winks at me as he takes the note and reads it. "I'll drop you at Lucy's house today," he says.

"Terrific!" I say. "Momma is meeting me there."

Lucy says, "We're painting my bedroom a new color today!"

"What color are you painting it?" Mr. Jim asks.

"My favorite color—purple!" Lucy replies.

Lucy and I take a seat and chat until the bus reaches Lucy's driveway.

"This is your stop, girls!" says Mr. Jim. "Have fun painting all that purple."

"Thanks, Mr. Jim!" we chime as we skip down the bus stairs and jump onto the pavement. Momma and Aunt Susie are waiting for us on the grass.

Aunt Susie waves and asks, "Are you ready to get to work, girls?"

"Yup!"

"Excellent!" says Aunt Susie. "First, go to my bedroom and change into your painting clothes."

"Yes, ma'am!"

Then we help carry the paint trays, brushes, and paint rollers down the hall to Lucy's room. Momma carries the paint cans. They are too HEAVY! Aunt Susie and Momma have laid painting cloths over the carpet to protect it from any spilled paint. The room is carefully outlined with blue painter's tape around the ceiling and baseboards.

Lucy looks at me and says, "I can't believe it! They think we're going to be messy painters!"

"Well . . . sometimes accidents do happen," I tell her.

Aunt Susie tells us to paint the low parts of the walls. Momma will paint the high parts, and Aunt Susie will paint all around the windows and corners. The shade of purple Lucy picked is the pale color of lilacs, just like the ones in Miss Clarabelle's yard. Even though we are trying to be careful, we still get paint on our faces, fingers, and in our hair. It seems like we are singing a little chorus of uh-ohs. I like painting in art class better. We use brushes and have a canvas or paper to paint on. But it is easier to paint with an art brush than a paint brush. Art brushes are smaller, and a canvas or paper is not as big as a wall!

Lucy says, "This paint makes us look like aliens."

"All we need is really big, green bug eyes and a spaceship!" I tell her.

Lucy, Momma, and Aunt Susie laugh.

"Aunt Susie, did you know I'm entering a painting contest?" I ask.

"I think Lucy mentioned it," she replies.

"If I win, they'll make my painting into a mural and paint it on a wall in our school," I explain.

Lucy asks, "Aren't you worried that an older kid will win?"

"Nope, I'm not worried. Mr. Lee says kids are natural artists, and that means we are all winners."

Aunt Susie asks, "Have you finished the painting you will enter into the contest?"

"I'm not sure," I tell her. "So far, my puppy portrait is my favorite. But it's not finished yet."

We paint until dinnertime. Right before we leave, I rush over to my backpack and pull out the pink pony painting. I hand it to Lucy.

Lucy gasps, "Is that for me?"

"It's for your room," I tell her.

She jumps up and down and hugs the pony painting. "Thank you!" she cries. "I love, love, love it! You know how much I love ponies!"

"You're welcome!" I reply. "I knew you'd love it."

We say our goodbyes, and Momma and I head home for dinner. Tonight is not a good night to finish my puppy portrait. I'm too worn out. I tell Momma that painting walls is not as much fun as painting pictures!

Georgia O'Keeffe is a famous American artist and a pioneer of modern art. She painted flowers, skyscrapers, and images from the Southwest.

Chapter Five
Pop Art Kylie

On Friday, I wake up early. It's still dark outside! I jump out of bed and tiptoe down the hall to the bathroom to fill a brush jar with water. In my room, Ugly Brother is still asleep on the end of the bed. When I shut the door, he opens one eye and grunts sleepily.

I whisper, "Go back to sleep, you sleepyhead."

I stand in front of my easel, looking at my painting of Ugly Brother.

First, I finish painting him. Then I'm ready to start the background of the farm. I paint the barn, then the trees, and then the sky and the grass. I make puffy clouds in the sky. With a dry brush, I paint over the green paint to make it look more like blades of grass. When I am nearly finished, I hear Momma.

"Breakfast!" she calls. "Hurry up, or you'll both be late for school."

"Coming, Momma," I shout.

Ugly Brother hears the word breakfast, jumps off the bed, and runs downstairs. He thinks he might get some bacon!

I get dressed quickly. Momma is waiting downstairs with my lunch bag, a breakfast bar, and a bottle of juice.

"The bus is going to be here any minute," she says. "You will have to eat fast."

I munch down the bar and gulp the juice.

Momma gives me a quick hug. "I'll pick you up after Art Club," she tells me.

Later at school, Lucy and I eat lunch with Ryder.

"I have decided to be a cowboy artist just like Remington," he tells us.

Lucy asks, "Do you think you'll be good at it?"

"Sure!" he replies. "I've been to lots of rodeos. I love the West."

"Looks like you've got it covered!" I say.

"I have a suggestion," says Lucy. "Why don't you visit our Uncle Bay's ranch and paint the cowboys and bulls."

"Really?" Ryder asks. "He'll let me?"

Ryder is very excited! He is going have his mom call Uncle Bay right after school.

The bell rings, and we all go out to recess. It's a beautiful fall day! I lie down in the grass and look at the clouds.

Lucy asks, "What are you doing?"

"Looking at nature is a wonderful way to get inspired," I tell her. "A lot of great artists paint deserts, oceans, and forests."

"Do you want to paint or play?" she asks. "It's recess time!"

I think for minute. Then I jump up for a game
of freeze tag.

****

After school, when we enter the art studio, there
are cans of soup on all the tables.

Ryder says, "YUM, I love soup!"

"Don't get too excited," Georgia tells him.
"We're not going to eat the soup."

"Georgia is right," says Mr. Lee. "We're going
to paint them!"

He shows us a slide show of paintings in bright
colors. We see shoes, soup cans, and portraits.
They're all painted in bright colors. Some are neon
orange, pink, turquoise, and lime green. The colors
are so fun!

"Andy Warhol painted these pieces," Mr. Lee tells us. "He became a famous pop artist in the 1960s. Pop art uses bold colors. Let's all paint a soup can today and experiment with pop art."

I can't wait! I bet you can guess what color I paint my soup can. If you guessed pink, you're right. Pink is my favorite color. My hot pink soup can turns out awesome!

Mr. Lee circles around the room looking at everyone's paintings. "Kylie Jean, I love your painting!" he says. "You have really embraced pop art with that bright pink color."

"Thanks, Mr. Lee," I say.

Then Mr. Lee turns to look at Ryder's brown painting. "Ryder, pop artists are known for using bright colors," he says.

Ryder says, "I know, but I'm into Western colors."

Mr. Lee nods his head. "Art is very personal, and you should paint what interests you," he says. "There are many shades of brown: chocolate, burnt umber, chestnut, tan, khaki, desert brown, russet, beige, tawny, mocha, and I could go on. There's a lot to like about the color brown!"

Ryder grins. Our art teacher is amazing! When it is almost time to go home, we gather at the front of the room. Mr. Lee asks what we are thinking about submitting for our mural contest entries.

Ryder says, "I'm painting a Western scene, and I hope it will have a bull in it!" Then he gives me a thumbs-up.

Georgia says, "I am very fond of painting portraits, and I have an idea about what I'd like to paint."

Some of the other kids also talk about what they are working on. One is painting the beach, and another is painting a scene at the city park. Just then I get a great idea! I decide to paint Lickskillet Farm. I just know a painting of my grandparents' farm will win the contest. It's my favorite place in the world!

Pop art is meant to be FUN! Pop artists use bold images and paint them in bright colors.

Chapter Six
Watercolor Washout

The next day is Saturday, and I have a plan!

"Momma, can we go to the farm?" I ask. "I need to go to paint something for Art Club."

"Can it wait until tomorrow when we all go for Sunday supper?" she asks.

"Too many people will be there on Sunday," I explain. "I will get distracted, and then I won't be able to paint my winning masterpiece."

Momma nods her head and says, "I see."

She calls Nanny to see if it will be okay for me to visit. Nanny will be home all day, so Momma tells Nanny that she will have T.J. drop me off before he goes to football practice.

Before Momma even hangs up the phone, I run upstairs to pack my paintbrushes and easel.

Ugly Brother wants to help me. He grabs my bag with his teeth.

"Would you like to go to the farm too?" I ask.

He barks, "Ruff, ruff." That means yes. He wants to go!

"Come on then," I say.

T.J. is waiting for us downstairs. He loads my easel into the back of his truck. Ugly Brother and my painting bag ride up front with me.

Ugly Brother gets excited when we turn onto the dirt road to the farm. Behind T.J.'s truck is a big dust cloud. When we get to the farmhouse, Nanny is working outside in her garden and walks over to greet us.

She asks, "What are you planning to paint, Kylie Jean?"

"I want to paint the pond with the barn behind it," I tell her. "The barn just makes me think of Lickskillet Farm."

Nanny asks, "Do you need anything?"

"Today I am painting with watercolor paint, so I will need a cup of water. And I could use help carrying my easel, please."

"Okay. I'll be right back!" Nanny says as she walks to the kitchen to get the water.

Ugly Brother runs around the yard chasing a butterfly. He loves visiting the farm! Nanny brings the water and carries my easel.

"I can't wait to see your masterpiece!" she says.

I set up my easel and fasten my art paper neatly under the clips. Then I add a little of the water to my watercolor tray. First I will brush my paper with water.

Mr. Lee already taught us how to paint with watercolor paint in art class. I paint the pond first. Dipping my brush in the blue paint, I swirl it around. Then I paint the center of the pond a deep indigo blue. By adding more water, I make the blue around the edges of the pond lighter. I stand back and look at my easel. I really like the way the color of the pond turned out.

Today the ducks are swimming near the tall grass.

"Ugly Brother, do you think I should paint the ducks?" I ask.

He barks, "Ruff, ruff."

That means yes! He is very excited about the ducks, so I paint them too.

Finally, it's time to paint the barn. It's just a giant square with a triangle on top. The rest of the painting is just details. I paint carefully to leave two white Xs on the barn doors. When you paint with watercolor, it's hard to use the color white. After a while, I step back and look at the barn. I like it!

"Ugly Brother, do you like my barn?" I ask. "Should I add a cow in a pen beside the barn?"

He barks, "Ruff, ruff!"

Yes. But then—

"RUFF!"

He changed his mind! That means I shouldn't paint a cow. This masterpiece is finished. I stand back and admire my work.

"Do you think my painting is a winner?" I ask Ugly Brother.

He knows that I'm dreaming of being an art queen. He barks excitedly over and over. I turn back to my painting and start to clean up. Suddenly I hear an awful racket.

"Quack, quaaack, QUACK!"

I turn around to see one of the ducks quacking and chasing Ugly Brother. They are running straight for my easel! Oh no!

A duck crashes right into the easel, and it starts to topple. My painting is still attached to it!

Behind him, Ugly Brother is running so fast, he can't stop. He runs into the easel and right into the cup of water, knocking it all over. OH NO! The water spills all over my painting!

"No!" I cry.

The duck is so scared, it runs away.

Ugly Brother sits down and hangs his head.

At first I want to sit down and cry. But I can't be mad at Ugly Brother. He is looking at me with big, sad puppy dog eyes. I know he feels really bad about the whole thing.

"It's okay," I tell him. "It was just an accident."

Then I start to notice something beautiful is happening to my painting. The paint wasn't dry yet, and the colors have begun to swirl across the paper. The barn disappears and becomes a large red circle. The sky and pond grow together, making a big, blue circle around the red circle. The ducks make small dots, and the grass makes green lines.

"Wow!" I shout. "Look at that."

Ugly Brother still feels bad. He just stares at my painting and then at me.

Nanny must have heard the racket too. She comes out to check on us. "Is everyone okay?" she asks. "I heard a lot of barking."

Then she sees my painting. "That's an unusual painting," she says.

"I know," I reply. "It wasn't before the accident."

While we pack up my art supplies and easel, I explain what happened. "I guess I have what we could call accidental art," I tell Nanny.

Nanny laughs. I can't wait to show this picture to Mr. Lee!

Abstract art is a form of art that has no subject.
It is just lines, shapes, and colors.

Chapter Seven
Abstract Kylie

On Monday I can't wait to take my accidental art to school to show Mr. Lee. As soon as I get on the bus, I show Mr. Jim my painting.

"What is it supposed to be?" he asks.

I explain, "You should just enjoy the colors in the picture."

"Okay," he says. "The colors are nice, but you need to sit down so I can drive you to school now."

Lucy pats the seat beside her. She's saving my spot! I sit down and tell her all about my accidental painting. Lucy cracks up at the part where Ugly Brother gets chased by a duck. She likes my painting too.

"I wonder what the Art Club kids will think of my painting?" I ask.

Lucy says, "You'll have to wait all day to find out."

When the bus pulls up to school, we shuffle off the bus and into the building. When it's finally lunchtime, I see Ryder.

He says, "Hi, Kylie Jean! How was your weekend? I painted all weekend."

"Hi, Ryder," I reply. "I painted all weekend too!"

"I painted a cowboy with your Uncle Bay's prize bull, Diablo," he tells me. "What did you paint?"

"I painted a farm," I explain. "At least, it was a farm, but then it wasn't."

"That's confusing," he says.

While we eat our sandwiches, I explain that something happened to my painting, but then I decided that I liked it better. The new picture is more interesting.

He says, "I can't wait to see it!"

After school when Ryder gets to the art studio, I'm showing Mr. Lee my painting.

"I love this painting," says Mr. Lee. "It's a great example of abstract art. Abstract art is all about colors, lines, and shapes. The colors in your painting are beautiful!"

"This is it!" I announce. "I want to use my abstract painting for the contest."

Ryder gives me a thumbs-up. Georgia and the other kids gather around. Everyone is talking about my painting.

Mr. Lee says, "Kylie Jean, you must have guessed that we're going to learn about abstract art today."

I just smile. Ryder smiles too. He knows that my painting is accidental abstract art. We look at several slides of abstract art. They are very colorful and full of shapes. One has a lot of colorful circles. They remind me of cupcakes. Maybe I'm hungry. Georgia says it looks a little like my painting, but I don't really think it does. It was painted by an artist named Kandinsky.

Mr. Lee has a rainbow of paint cups waiting for us to use in creating our abstract art. I sure hope he has pink! When I find the cup of pink paint, I'm ready to get started. We all get to work painting. Mr. Lee is playing music. It sounds like jazz, and I like it.

Closing my eyes, I listen. I can imagine that the different notes have different colors. The soft ones are pale pink, the strong ones are black, the long ones are blue, and the repeating notes are red. I open my eyes and begin to paint using pink, black, blue, and red.

Mr. Lee says, "You can't go wrong! Just jump in and paint shapes and colors."

No one wants to stop painting, but soon it's time for the club to end.

"I have an announcement!" says Mr. Lee. "On Wednesday, everyone will need to bring their paintings for the Gallery Art Walk and the mural contest judging on Friday."

Wassily Kandinsky was an abstract artist who could hear color and see sound.

Chapter Eight
Show and Tell

On Wednesday at Art Club, Mr. Lee talks about
the famous mural painter Diego Rivera. We look
at slides of his murals. He painted many murals
in Mexico and around the world. I like the one
of the lady holding a big bunch of white flowers.
Then Mr. Lee asks each of us to stand, show our
painting, and talk about why we chose it for the
contest. Georgia has painted a portrait just like
Frida. It's beautiful!

She says, "I chose this painting because painting portraits makes me happy."

Everyone claps!

"Your painting is vibrant," says Mr. Lee. "Your use of color is powerful. Well done, Georgia!"

Then it's my turn. I'm not nervous. I like Mr. Lee, and the kids in Art Club are my friends.

"This my painting," I explain. "I've named it Barn with Ducks. Some of you have already heard the story of my painting, and some of you have not. This is an accidental piece of abstract art. I finished painting it, but before it could dry, my doggie brother and duck got into a tussle and tipped a cup of water onto it. The water swirled around and made this lovely abstract picture."

"Your story is very interesting, and your painting will be the only abstract one in the contest," says Mr. Lee. "Way to go, Kylie Jean!"

One by one, all the kids show their paintings and tell us about them. Finally, Ryder is the only kid left.

He says, "This is my Western painting of a cowboy with a bull. I couldn't have painted it without the help of Kylie Jean's uncle. He let me visit his ranch. And Mr. Lee taught me how to mix all the shades of brown in this painting!"

"Bravo!" Georgia shouts.

We all clap and clap. Ryder's painting is fantastic!

Mr. Lee says, "You are all fine artists! It will be difficult for the judges to decide. Please invite your parents to come on Friday to the Gallery Art Walk."

While we have our snack, we talk about how exciting it would be to win the contest.

"If I won, I'd be a real, true art queen," I tell my friends.

"You are a real, true artist," says Mr. Lee, "and I think that makes you an art queen already."

"Thank you!" I gush. "That makes me happy!"

Soon Momma picks me up from Art Club, and I tell her about the Gallery Art Walk. Momma says we are having company for dinner. Our neighbor Miss Clarabelle will be our guest. We're having fried chicken and biscuits for dinner. My favorite!

When the doorbell rings, I answer it. "Hello, Miss Clarabelle!" I sing. "Please come in and join us in the kitchen."

"Thank you, sweet girl," replies Miss Clarabelle.

She steps into the kitchen and smells the chicken. "That fried chicken smells heavenly, and it's my favorite dinner."

Miss Clarabelle loves Momma's fried chicken!

"I love it too!" I tell her.

While Momma and Miss Clarabelle chat about the fried chicken recipe, I set the table. T.J. and Daddy come in to help. Momma asks them to bring the food to the table. They carry out a big steamy bowl of mashed potatoes, a platter of golden fried chicken, a small bowl of white gravy with a swirl of black pepper on top, and buttery green beans. I get to carry a big basket of hot biscuits. We sit down, say grace, and dish up our plates.

As we eat, I tell Miss Clarabelle all about the mural art contest. "I really want to win and be an art queen, but there are a lot of awesome artists in my club. Mr. Lee, my teacher, told me I can be an art queen anyway since I'm already an artist."

Miss Clarabelle smiles and says, "I like Mr. Lee. He sounds smart and nice."

Daddy dishes up apple pie for dessert. It's delicious!

Then I ask, "Miss Clarabelle, would you like to visit my studio?"

"I adore art," she says. "I'd love to see your studio."

Upstairs, Miss Clarabelle's eyes get big. She gasps and claps her hands together when she sees all of my paintings!

"I really like the pink ones, since pink is my favorite color," I explain. "But I also have some other favorites. Which one is your favorite?"

"That portrait of Ugly Brother is my favorite," she replies. "I love dogs! Your painting shows his personality. It should be in a gallery!"

Then Miss Clarabelle gets a twinkle in her eye. She has an idea, but it will be a surprise. She asks me to send her a picture of the puppy portrait. I'm curious now. I wonder what the surprise is going to be.

Diego Rivera was one of Mexico's most famous artists and muralists. As a child, he painted on his parents' walls.

Chapter Nine
Gallery Walk

On Friday, I wake up with a stomach full of butterflies. Today is the big day! After school is the Gallery Walk, and the judges will pick a winner!

Downstairs, Momma and Daddy have a special breakfast waiting for me—cinnamon rolls!

"Only art queens have studios," Daddy tells me.

"You are an amazing artist!" Momma says.

"Aww . . . thanks," I reply. "I love you!"

I get a big icy glass of milk to go with my roll. I finish just in time to see my bus coming down my street. Mr. Jim doesn't need to honk the horn. I'm waiting on the sidewalk in no time. When I get on the bus, I sit by my best cousin, Lucy.

She says, "Today you're going to find out who won the contest. Right?"

"Yes!"

"Good luck, cousin!" she adds.

"Thanks, Lucy!" I reply.

All day I'm wondering who will win the contest. I have trouble concentrating on math, my mind wanders during reading time, and I don't even get excited about our science experiment. We already did one like it in first grade.

Finally, the bell rings. I hug Lucy goodbye and tell her I'll call her later. Then I head to the art room.

Mr. Lee has tall black screens set up throughout the school with our paintings displayed on them. Before long, Momma and Daddy come, and we start our gallery walk. I see them looking at Ryder's painting.

Momma says, "This painting is wonderful!"

Daddy agrees. "I like all the brown colors," he says.

I see two men and a lady wearing tags that say "Judge." They all have clipboards so they can make notes about each painting. The judges are an art teacher from the college, a high school art teacher, and an artist who is a photographer.

I whisper, "Momma, look. The judges are here."

Momma and Daddy are still looking at Ryder's picture.

"Did one of your friends paint this one?" Daddy asks.

"Yes, I'll introduce him to you," I reply.

I start looking for Ryder, but I don't see him right away. When I finally spot him, I wave him over.

"This is my friend Ryder," I announce. "Ryder, this is my momma and daddy."

Ryder sticks out his hand. "Nice to meet you," he says.

"Nice to meet you, Ryder," Daddy says as he shakes his hand.

"Your painting is beautiful," Momma tells him.

Ryder blushes a bit. "Thanks so much," he replies.

We continue to walk around and look at the paintings. But I'm distracted. I can't wait for the judges to look at my painting! This waiting is making me more nervous.

They look at Ryder's painting for a long time. Ryder's mom and dad look anxious. Ryder looks excited.

The judges continue to look at the paintings and make notes. When they finally get to my painting, I notice that they are making a lot of notes.

"Momma, do you think I'll win the contest?" I ask.

"Your picture is my favorite," she replies. "But we'll have to wait and see what the judges say."

Mr. Lee invites everyone into the art studio for refreshments while the judges place the ribbons on the paintings. All the parents and kids gather around the big art table for punch and cookies. We laugh, talk, and enjoy the snacks.

Soon the judges join us, and Mr. Lee says he has a special announcement to make. Everyone gets quiet. We are all listening to find out who will be the winner. I am crossing my fingers and holding my breath. I really want to be an art queen.

"The first place winner of the contest is Ryder Nelson!" says Mr. Lee.

A big smile crawls across Ryder's face. His mom and dad hug him and shake hands with the judges. He gets a blue ribbon, and his painting will be made into a mural for the school.

Everyone is congratulating Ryder. And he looks so happy!

I give him a high five. "Your painting deserved to win."

"Thanks," he says. "I liked your painting too."

I see Georgia, and she looks excited. She hurries over and says that she heard the judges talking, and there are still more prizes to give away.

Just then, Mr. Lee says, "Some of our paintings have received red honorable mention ribbons. Congratulations to Kylie Jean and Georgia!"

Everyone cheers! Momma and Daddy hug me.

"I'm so proud of you, sugar!" Daddy says. "You are so creative."

On the way home, I tell Momma she was right. As long as I'm an artist, I'll always be an art queen!

Kylie Jean Carter, prize-winning kid artist
who is known for use of pink paint.

Chapter Ten
Minimalist Kylie Jean

The next day is Saturday morning, and the mural art contest is over. I look around my room at all the paintings covering my walls. Each one is special to me, but I can't keep them all. Mr. Lee says art is meant to be shared.

Downstairs, Daddy is making pancakes, so I head down to join him. T.J. and Momma are helping him.

"Are you sad you didn't win, Lil' Bit?" asks T.J.

"No," I reply. "It's hard to be sad that I didn't win, because I'm so excited for Ryder. He's a second grader, just like me, and he won!"

Just then we hear a knock on the back door. It's Miss Clarabelle.

"Come on in," Momma chimes.

Miss Clarabelle speaks quietly to Momma. Momma has a giant grin on her face.

"Miss Clarabelle has some BIG news," Momma announces.

"What is it?" I ask.

"Your puppy portrait has been selected for the Jacksonville Library Art Exhibit!" says Miss Clarabelle.

My mouth drops open in surprise.

Miss Clarabelle continues, "Fifty local artists will have paintings, sculptures, photos, and quilts exhibited in the library for the next two weeks."

"Really?" I ask. "Yippee!"

Momma shouts, "Hooray!"

"Congratulations, sugar!" Daddy says.

"Good work, little sister," T.J. tells me.

Ugly Brother jumps and barks. He's super excited for me!

"Good art always finds a way to be seen," says Miss Clarabelle.

I give her a big squeezy hug. "This is the best surprise ever! Thank you for telling the library about my artwork. I want you to have the puppy portrait after the art exhibit is over."

"Oh, you sweet girl, I can't accept such a valuable gift," she says. "The painting of Ugly Brother is a precious treasure!"

"You have to take the painting, Miss Clarabelle," I insist. "I'm going to be giving away almost all of my paintings."

Daddy is adding chocolate chips to the pancakes. He thinks we need to celebrate.

I watch Daddy stack the flipped pancakes on a blue platter. They are golden brown and dotted with little chocolate freckles. I can't wait to eat them dripping with maple syrup and with a tall frosty glass of milk.

Momma asks, "Are you tired of being an artist?"

"No, not at all," I tell her. "But I'm going to try minimalism next, and minimal artists don't need a lot to create their art. They keep things simple."

Momma and Miss Clarabelle both smile.

Momma says, "You know something . . . Kylie Jean, you are simply my favorite artist. And you truly are an art queen!"

Minimalism is a simple form of modern art
that uses geometric shapes.

Marci Bales Peschke was born in Indiana, grew up in Florida, and now lives in Texas with her husband, two children, and a cat named Cookie. She loves reading and watching movies.

When **Tuesday Mourning** was a little girl, she knew she wanted to be an artist when she grew up. Now, she is an illustrator who lives in Utah. She especially loves illustrating books for kids and teenagers. When she isn't illustrating, Tuesday loves spending time with her husband, who is an actor, and their two sons and one daughter.

Glossary

canvas (CAN-vass)—a piece of cloth framed as a surface for painting

exhibit (ig-ZI-buht)—a display that shows something to the public

gallery (GAL-uh-ree)—a place where art is shown

inspiration (in-spihr-AY-shun)—something that fills someone with an emotion, idea, or attitude

landscape (LAND-skape)—a picture that shows the natural scenery in an area

masterpiece (MAS-tur-pees)—an artist's work done with great skill

modern artist (MAH-dern ART-ist)—someone who created art during the time period from the 1860s to the 1970s

retreat (ree-TREET)—a period of group time to teach a certain skill

palette (PA-let)—a thin oval or rectangular board an artist holds to mix colors on

portrait (POR-trit)—a picture of someone, usually showing the face

submit (sub-MIT)—to send something for a review or decision

Talk!

1. Kylie Jean learns about many famous artists. Ask an adult to help you research famous artists online. Which one is your favorite and why? Talk with a friend about your favorite artist.

2. When Kylie Jean's painting is ruined, she makes the best of it. Can you think of a time when something you made was ruined? What could you have done to make the best of it?

3. What kind of mural would you like to create? Talk about your answer with a friend. Imagine how you could work together to create a beautiful mural!

Be Creative!

1. Kylie Jean learned about modern art, abstract art, pop art, and others. Ask an adult to help you research different kinds of art. Pick one style and paint your own picture!

2. Now that you have your own painting, take a look and find places to add even more details. Can you add some other colors? Choose a name for your painting. Show your painting to a friend or family member and explain how you created it.

3. Write a short story about your painting. Are there other characters or images you can create to go with the story? Paint those too!

This is the perfect craft and treat for any art queen!
Just make sure to ask a grown-up for help.

Love, Kylie Jean

From Momma's Kitchen

Hand-Painted Mugs and Pink Cocoa

YOU NEED:

- white mugs
- rubbing alcohol
- oil-based markers
- 2 tablespoons cocoa
- 1 tablespoon chocolate chips
- 2 tablespoons sugar

- $\frac{1}{4}$ cup water
- 2 cups milk
- $\frac{1}{4}$ teaspoon vanilla
- whipped cream topping
- pink sprinkles

1. Wipe down the mug(s) with rubbing alcohol.
2. Draw a fun design on your mug with the markers.
3. Place the mug(s) on a cookie sheet, and place in a cold oven.
4. Allow oven to preheat to 350 degrees F. Bake for 30 minutes.
5. Cool in the oven, and make sure you let the mug(s) cool thoroughly before touching them. They'll be hot for a few hours. Wash the mug(s) before making pink cocoa.
6. Combine cocoa, chocolate chips, sugar, and water in a mug. Microwave for 30 seconds, then stir. Microwave for another 30 seconds, or until the chocolate chips are completely melted. Stir well.
7. Slowly add milk and vanilla. Stir, and heat for one to two minutes, or until hot. Top with whipped topping and sprinkles!

Yum, yum!

THE FUN DOESN'T STOP HERE!

Discover more at www.capstonekids.com

- ♥ Videos & Contests
- ✿ Games & Puzzles
- ♥ Friends & Favorites
- ✿ Authors & Illustrators

Find cool websites and more books like this one at www.facthound.com. Just type in the Book ID: **9781515829270** and you're ready to go!